A NOTE TO PARENTS

Reading Aloud with Your Child

Research shows that reading books aloud is the single most valuable support parents can provide in helping children learn to read.

- Be a ham! The more enthusiasm you display, the more your child will enjoy the book.
- Run your finger underneath the words as you read to signal that the print carries the story.
- Leave time for examining the illustrations more closely; encourage your child to find things in the pictures.
- Invite your youngster to join in whenever there's a repeated phrase in the text.
- Link up events in the book with similar events in your child's life.
- If your child asks a question, stop and answer it. The book can be a means to learning more about your child's thoughts.

Listening to Your Child Read Aloud

The support of your attention and praise is absolutely crucial to your child's continuing efforts to learn to read.

- If your child is learning to read and asks for a word, give it immediately so that the meaning of the story is not interrupted. DO NOT ask your child to sound out the word.
- On the other hand, if your child initiates the act of sounding out, don't intervene.
- If your child is reading along and makes what is called a miscue, listen for the sense of the miscue. If the word "road" is substituted for the word "street," for instance, no meaning is lost. Don't stop the reading for a correction.
- If the miscue makes no sense (for example, "horse" for "house"), ask your child to reread the sentence because you're not sure you understand what's just been read.
- Above all else, enjoy your child's growing command of print and make sure you give lots of praise. *You are your child's first teacher—and the most important one. Praise from you is critical for further risk-taking and learning.*

—Priscilla Lynch
Ph.D., New York University
Educational Consultant

For Ralph and Tillie,
who already know how to dance.
—T.S.

For my son Larson.
—L.D.

Library of Congress Cataloging-in-Publication Data

Slater, Teddy,
    The bunny hop / by Teddy Slater, illustrated by Larry Di Fiori.
       p.   cm.—(Hello reader)
    Summary: Buddy Rabbit is ignored by the girls because of his incompetent dancing, until he masters the bunny hop.
    ISBN 0-590-45354-8
    [1. Rabbit—Fiction.   2. Dancing—Fiction.]   I. Di Fiori, Lawrence, ill. II. Title. III. Series.
PZ7.S6294Bv   1992
[E]—dc20
                                                    91-19715
                                                     CIP
                                                     AC

12   4 5 6/9

Printed in the U.S.A.   23

First Scholastic printing, March 1992

The Bunny Hop

by Teddy Slater • Illustrated by Larry Di Fiori

Hello Reader!—Level 1

SCHOLASTIC INC. Cartwheel B·O·O·K·S™

New York Toronto London Auckland Sydney

Chapter 1
Nine Dancing Bunnies

One bunny,
two bunnies,
three bunnies . . .

HOP!

Four bunnies,

five bunnies,

six bunnies . . .
HOP!

Seven bunnies,

eight bunnies,

nine bunnies . . .

STOP!

It's best to have
ten bunnies
when you do
the Bunny Hop!

Chapter 2
The Tenth Bunny

This is Buddy Rabbit.
He never learned to dance.

His great big feet
got in the way.
He never had a chance.

Wanda would not
waltz with him.

Neither would Belinda.

Becky said, "Forget it, Bud!"
"No way!" said Melinda.

Buddy could not jitterbug.

He could not even fox-trot.

He could not do
the cha-cha-cha.
He could not,
could not, could not!

"Ow! Yow! Zow!"
the girls all cried.
"You're stepping
on our toes!"

"Ouch! Youch! Zouch!"
they yelled out loud.

"How can you
dance with those?"

Poor Buddy sat down
all alone.
Then he began to cry.
"I was not born
to dance," he said.
"I might as well not try."

Chapter 3
Buddy Learns to Dance

One day Buddy
heard a sound.
It drove him from his seat.
Thumpity-thump, thump.
Bumpity-bump.

A bunny-hopping beat!

Thumpity-thump.
His ears were flapping.
Bumpity-bump.
His toes were tapping.

Bud flapped and tapped
to the back of the line.
That didn't work at all.

He hippity-hopped
right up
to the front.

Then he
had a ball!

One and two
and three...
HOP!

One and two
and three.

"One, two, three,"
Bud sang out loud.

"I'm dancing!
Look at me!"